Агустус и его улыбка

Augustus and his Smile

Text and Illustrations copyright © Catherine Rayner 2006
Catherine Raynor has asserted her right to be identified as the author and
illustrator of this work under the Copyright, Designs and Patents Act, 1988
Dual language copyright © Mantra Lingua 2008
Printed Paola, Malta MP210217PB03171891

Mantra Lingua
303 Ballards Lane, London N12 8NP
www.mantralingua.com

First published in UK
by Little Tiger Press 2006
This edition published 2017

Audio copyright ©
Mantra Lingua 2008

Thank you, Mum, Brian and Colin - C R

Агустус и его улыбка

Augustus and his Smile

Catherine Rayner

Russian translation by
Dr Lydia Buravova

MANTRA
LINGUA

Тигр Агустус был очень расстроен.
Он потерял свою улыбку.

Augustus the tiger was sad.
He had lost his smile.

Он СИЛЬНО потянулся и отправился на ее поиски.

So he did a HUGE tigery stretch and set off to find it.

Сначала он рыскал в зарослях кустов. Там он нашел маленького блестящего жучка, но не смог найти своей улыбки.

First he crept under a cluster of bushes. He found a small, shiny beetle, but he couldn't see his smile.

Then he climbed to the tops of the tallest trees.
He found birds that chirped and called,
but he couldn't find his smile.

Потом он карабкался на верхушки самых высоких деревьев.
Он любовался чирикающими и щебечущими птицами,
но не смог найти своей улыбки.

Все дальше и дальше брел Агустус.
Он взбирался на вершины самых высоких гор, туда,
где кружились снежные облака, рисуя ледяные узоры
в морозном воздухе.

Further and further Augustus searched.
He scaled the crests of the highest mountains where the snow
clouds swirled, making frost patterns in the freezing air.

Он опускался на дно самых глубоких океанов
и резвился, и плескался со стаями крошечных
сверкающих рыбок.

He swam to the bottom of the deepest oceans and
splished and splashed with shoals of tiny, shiny fish.

Он мчался по бескрайней пустыне, играя с
причудливыми тенями.
Бесшумно бежал Агустус все дальше
и дальше
сквозь зыбучие пески
пока …

He pranced and paraded through
the largest desert, making
shadow shapes in the sun.
Augustus padded further
and further
through shifting sand
until …

... pitter patter

pitter patter

drip

drop.

plop!

... шлёп шлёп

шлёп шлёп

кап

кап

буль!

Агустус танцевал
и резвился
под летящими и
прыгающими
каплями дождя.

Augustus danced
and raced
as raindrops bounced
and flew.

Он шлепал по лужам, большим и глубоким.
Он помчался к огромной серебристо-голубой луже
и увидел …

He splashed through puddles, bigger and deeper.
He raced towards a huge silver-blue puddle
and saw …

… прямо у себя под носом
… свою улыбку!

… there under his nose
… his smile!

И тут Агустус понял, что его улыбка будет на этом самом месте всякий раз, когда он будет весел.
Все что ему для этого нужно – так только плавать с рыбками, или шлёпать по лужам, или карабкаться по горам и смотреть на мир, потому что счастье – всегда рядом с ним.

Агустус был так счастлив, что прыгал
и скакал …

And Augustus realised that his smile would be there, whenever he was happy.

He only had to swim with the fish or dance in the puddles, or climb the mountains and look at the world – for happiness was everywhere around him.

Augustus was so pleased that
he hopped
and skipped …

… и умчался вдаль,
улыбаясь.

… and jumped away,
smiling.

Amazing tiger facts
Augustus is a Siberian tiger.
Siberian tigers are the biggest cats in the world! They live in Southern Russia and Northern China where the winters are very cold.
Most tigers are orange with black stripes. The stripes make them hard to see when they walk through tall weeds and grasses.
Tigers are good swimmers and like to cool down by sitting in waterholes.
Each tiger's stripes are different to those of other tigers – like a human finger print.

Tigers are in danger …
Tigers are only hunted by one animal … HUMANS!And humans are ruining the land on which tigers live.
There are more tigers living in zoos and nature reserves than in the wild. There are only about 6000 tigers left in the wild.

Help save the tiger!

World Wildlife Fund (WWF)
 Panda House
 Weyside Park
 Godalming
 Surrey GU7 1XR
 Tel: 01483 426 444
 www.wwf.org.uk

David Shepherd Wildlife Foundation
61 Smithbrook Kilns
Cranleigh
Surrey GU76 8JJ
Tel: 01483 727 323/267 924
www.davidshepherd.org